Friendly

Early one fine Saturday morning, I got out of bed, freshen up and strolled to the kitchen. When my eyes landed on delicious Emily in a short ass nightgown.

Damn she looked fine as hell and I couldn't resist her feminine charms anymore. I embraced her from behind. I said how is the goddess of Manhattan doing today.

Emily giggled as I kissed her beautiful neck, grinding my morning wood into her juicy fine ass. I cupped her melons; she moaned with pleasure and grind her sexy ass into my hard cock.

Emily said is that your huge black cock or you just happy to see me. I said both and she laughed out loud. I reached down south to rub her pussy and she was not wearing any panties.

I massaged her white pussy, Emily moaned and said damn your making me wet and horny. I said a vanilla goddess should always be wet and horny. I lifted up her dress and dropped my boxers. I grind my bare black cock on her bare white juicy ass.

Emily said stick that big black cock in my little white pussy if you can get it in. I tried and tried, she said damn you have a big cock. I pushed harder and my black cock went in her pussy forcefully.

I started pumping and feeling way too good. Emily said damn your huge cock feels so good in my tight pussy. I said tell me about it as I pumped her white pussy full of black cock.

Emily said yes here is comes as she creamed my black dick. I said oh yeah, I love making a white girl cream. Emily said your big dick is very pleasurable.

Emma walked in and said oh my god Emily you have a boyfriend. Emily said I'm sorry don't rat me out bestie. Emma said I won't. Emily said show her. I took my cock out and spanked Emily's juicy ass with my hard-black cock coated with Emily's fresh pleasure cream.

Emma said damn boy no wonder you let him fuck your white pussy with that big black thing. Emily said now you know. I pushed my cock back into Emily's wet pussy.

I pounded the shit out of her as Emma watched. Emily creamed my dick one more time before I filled her heaven with a cloud of pleasure.

I said thanks Emily after I came in her. I kissed her passionately feeling on her sexy ass. I turned to Emma and said that's one fine ass white girl and a great fuck.

Both Emma and Emily laughed out loud. I walked out of the room but I stopped to listen where they couldn't see me. Emma said how was that, Emily said amazing I never came so many times when I guy fucks me.

Emma said his big cock had something to do with it, I bet he creates orgasms every time he fucks a white girl. Emily said I'm living proof of it and they both giggled. I walked away smiling and happy.

A month later, I was up late with Emma. She was looking fucking amazing. It was just her and me at home. Emily was over at her boyfriend for the weekend.

Emma cuddled up to me as we watched late night television. I held her and started rubbing her sweet white thighs. I told her I love your fucking sweet white thighs. Emma giggled then I kissed her as I felt on her big titties.

Emma started rubbing my dick so I spread her sweet white thighs and rubbed her white pussy. I slid my middle finger in her pussy. Her wet pussy spurred me on so I climbed on top of her.

Emma spread her sweet white thighs and said fuck me with your huge black cock. I held it and tried to push it in, no dice, I spread her wider and used more force. I was in like sin and started pumping.

Emma started enjoying it more than me, five minutes later she screamed oh fuck I'm coming baby. I gave it to her harder and she fucking came again. I thought oh my god her pussy is so good.

I said bend over I want to smack that juicy ass of yours. Emma bent over giggling. I smacked her ass and she love it. She said pull my hair and give it to me. I pulled her long blonde hair and gave her what she wanted. A proper roman pounding.

Emma gave up the cream twice as I took her doggie before I spilled the beans in her proper roman cunt. I said you are a proper roman fuck baby and Emma said thanks big daddy.

We cuddled up and made out for a while. I said don't worry, I'll keep this a secret from Emily and your boyfriend. Emma said no wonder we get along so well. I smiled and gave her a peck on the lips.

Unfortunately, the next day Emma had to work. Emma and Emily are both pharmacist and I'm a bank manager. We live in a sweet luxury apartment in Manhattan, New York.

I chilled until both of them came back late Sunday. I hugged them both goodnight as usual and went to bed. We ate breakfast together Monday morning and I could feel the sexual tension between all three of us.

The following weekend, they told me that they are spending it with their boyfriends so I was going to be all alone. So, I got all dressed up and went to a club. I was chilling in the corner when this curvy goddess came up to me asked if I was here alone.

I said yeah why, she said dance with me. I said sure sexy. She giggled and we started dancing. Her name was Erin and she gave me a boner immediately grinding on my cock.

I dug her right away. When she felt my cock, she said sweet fuck that big cock feels good on my pussy. I kissed her passionately and grabbed her juicy ass.

Erin pushed me against the wall and we sucked face for a long time. When we came up for air, we went back to dancing. I turned her around putting her on the wall. I worked her big booty over and felt up her big titties.

Erin leaned back and said I love your big hands all over me. She reached for my cock so I let her stroke it for a while. When she had enough, she asked if I wanted to fuck her tonight.

I said hell yeah, I want to tear that white pussy up. Erin said that is great to hear. She took me by the hand and introduced me to her two hot sisters and their husbands. I shook the husbands hands while the sisters gave me warm hugs with their sexy curvy bodies.

Erin told them that she was going home with me tonight. They left and I took Erin back to my place. She said where is your bedroom that is when I told her I have two roommates.

Erin said are they home. I said no they are with their boyfriends for the weekend. Erin said so I can scream when you put it on me. I said sure. I took her to my room.

She pushed me against the door and kissed me passionately as I felt up her big booty. Erin drop to her knees and ripped my pants off. She engulfed my black cock with her wonderful mouth.

She sucked me amazingly well as I held her pretty head. After a little while, I said my turn and tossed her on the bed. I spread her sweet white thighs and went to work on her clit. It drove her nuts after a little bit she said fuck me big daddy.

I looked her in her pretty eyes and slammed my cock up her wet cunt. She screamed with pleasure as I gave it to her. Erin held me tight digging into my back as I pounded her balls deep.

She took it really well creaming the hell out of my cock. I bent her over and took her from behind. I smacked her juicy booty as I fucked her silly. I ejaculated all of my seed in her horny pussy. We fell to the bed as I kissed her neck massaging her melons.

We cuddled up and talked for a while. My roommates came up and she asked if they were male or female. I told her female and she said interesting. I spooned her and we went to sleep.

I woke up early and made her breakfast in bed. Erin smiled and said this is a first for me. I said wow I'm glad I thought of it. Erin gave me a big warm smile and ate her breakfast.

She kissed me and said thank you baby. I'm glad I ran into you at the club. I said me too. We hung out all weekend and fucked each other's brains out.

When Emma and Emily came back, I introduced them to Erin. She hugged both of them said wow, you have hot roommates. Both Emma and Emily turned red.

The following weekend, Erin came over, we were in bed hanging out. When out of the blue, she asked if I fucked my roommates. I said you can't tell anyone but I fucked both of them even though they have boyfriends.

I told her Emma knows I fucked Emily because she caught us fucking in the kitchen. But Emily does not know that I fucked Emma. Erin said wow that's juicy. I said please don't bring it up they would be mortified.

Erin said I love keeping secrets that is so erotic, you are boning both of your hot roommates with your big black cock. I took a nap for a few hours. I woke up and Erin was on the couch with Emma and Emily chatting it up like besties.

I said break it up what's going on here. Emma and Emily said just getting to know your new girlfriend. She is a riot and a she is a fine newspaper editor. I took her home a day later and came back.

Emma and Emily said your girlfriend is wonderful and she likes us. I said I'm happy my three hotties get along just fine. They laughed out loud.

A month later, Erin had four tickets to a Jay Z and Beyoncé concert. Erin asked Emily and Emma if they wanted to go. They said hell yeah. So, we went to the concert together, we had a private suite.

I grind on Erin during the concert while Emily and Emma danced with each other. Erin whispered in my ears then went to the bathroom.

I said come here you two, time to dance with me. We started grinding on each other. It was pretty hot as both felt my hard-black cock on their white pussies and juicy asses for a while. Erin buzzed my cell phone. So, I stopped dancing with both of them.

The door opened and I went back to dancing with Erin. Emma and Emily went back to dancing with each other. It was a great concert and we all enjoyed ourselves along with great music.

Monday at work Emma texted thanks for dancing with me at the concert, you made me wet. I replied my pleasure hot stuff. Emily texted me too thanks for grinding on my pussy at the concert. I said I hope I made you wet. Emily replied, you always make me wet lol.

I went home feeling good. Emily and Emma were both sitting on the couch in short skirts. I said oh my god you two have some sweet ass white thighs. Both blushed and gave me warm hugs welcoming me home. I felt up both of their juicy booties when I hugged them.

It is Friday night and all three of us were on the couch. I started rubbing Emily's sweet white thighs then her big titties. She kissed me passionately and I reciprocated her action.

Emily took my dick out and got between my legs. She took out her melons and I put my black cock between her white melons. She tit fucked my black cock. Emma said oh my god you two are two horndogs.

Emily said sorry Emma, I can't help it our roommate knows how to press my sexual buttons. I asked Emma if her pussy is wet. She said yeah, with Emily fucking your huge cock, the contrast is intoxicating me.

Emily stood up held my cock and slid down my black pole. It felt wonderful being in her warm inviting pussy. I sucked her big titties as she rode my cock slowly. I squeezed her ass too.

I heard a moan next to us. We both looked over at Emma. She was squeezing both her big fucking titties and biting her lips. I said are you horny Emma. She said yeah you two fucking right next to me got me in the mood.

Emily went back to riding my cock harder. She moaned and threw her head back in ecstasy as she creamed my black bone. Emma said did you cum Emily. Emily said fuck yeah all over his big fucking cock.

I moaned loudly and spilled my seed in Emily's horny pussy. She kissed me passionately as we came down from our sexual highs. Emma said that was fucking hot, black cock balls deep in white pussy.

Emily asked Emma if she liked watching us fuck and she said oh yeah, every second of it. I hugged Emily and kissed her good night. I hugged and felt up Emma's ass good night.

I laid in bed can't believing what just happened. I got a text from Emma. She said I'm still horny would you like some more white pussy tonight. I said hell yeah where. She said come to my room quietly.

I snuck into Emma's room, she was naked and ready for cock. She said thanks for coming with a big smile on her face. I climbed in her bed and onto Emma. We kissed like long lost lovers. It was fucking intense.

Emma moaned in my ears as I kissed her neck. Then she said fuck me like you did Emily. I mounted Emma ramming my cock in her horny pussy. I started slamming her white pussy full of black cock.

Emma moaned oh god I love your black cock then she creamed my cock. I felt the extra lubrication. I said bend over sweet cheeks. I penetrated her from behind. I held her hips and went after my orgasm. Emma loved it, I felt her pussy vibrate and saw her love juice.

I sped up my pumping and filled up her lusty pussy with my pleasure cream. We made out for a long time. I said I can't believe I boned both of my roommates tonight. Emma said your cream is in both of our horny white pussies.

I said I better get back to my room before Emily catches us. Emma said I really appreciate you coming to my room to fuck me in secret. I said my pleasure hot Emma. She turned red then said time for your walk of shame back to your bedroom. I smiled and said it's the most pleasurable walk of shame ever.

I went back to my room and fell asleep tired from fucking both of my roommates. I woke up and went to the kitchen. Emma and Emily were both up, they said we made you breakfast.

I said thanks roomies. I hugged and kissed Emily and I hugged Emma. She whispered in my ears thanks for last night stud. I sat down and ate breakfast with Emma and Emily like everything was normal except that my sperm was in both of their tight white vaginas.

My girlfriend Erin came over and I was very happy to see her. We went to my room to hang out. I spread her sweet white thighs and took her red panties off. I kissed her sweet white thighs then chewed on her clit. Erin held my head and said oh boy I'm glad I came over.

Erin moaned out loud, I'm sure Emma and Emily heard. I held my hard cock and plunged it into Erin's wet pussy. I kissed her hard and fucked her harder. She held on for dear life and I fucked the shit out of her.

Erin moaned oh god as she creamed my cock. She said I love my black boyfriend as I gave her the business. Erin held me tight never letting go but I had to let go of my sperm in her tight ass white vagina.

I kissed her as we held each other after vigorous coitus on my part. Erin said oh wow that was very strong love making what has gotten into you. I said nothing just very happy to see my hot girlfriend.

Erin said I'm not buying it, so I told her I boned both Emily and Erin last night. I told her everything that happened. Erin said oh wow, you creamed both of their pussies and still had cock for me. She said your girlfriend is very impress at your stamina. I smiled and kissed her on her luscious lips.

Erin said I need to hug both of them since we are now stick sisters officially. I said are you going to tell them. Erin said hell no I love keeping secrets. We went out to the living room. Both Emily and Emma were sitting and watching television.

They got up when they saw us. Erin hugged Emily and then Emma. Erin said can I take you guys to dinner. I was surprised when Emily and Emma said ok. We got dress and went to a fancy restaurant.

We were seated and three of my girls were showing off the big titties. My cock was hard and I couldn't help but drool. The big tit waitress came over and said hi I'm Megan and gave us menus.

A few minutes later the waitress came back with our drinks. Megan said there is a lot of titties at this table including mine. I laughed out loud, so did Erin, Emma and Emily. It broke the ice and then Megan said what can I get you guys.

We ordered out meals and Megan said it will be 15 minutes. She said I hope you don't mind me asking is he banging all three of you girls. Erin said no he is just banging me. I'm his white girl and these two are his roommates.

Megan said oh wow lucky guy, you must have a huge cock. Erin said he does and it has giving me many orgasms in fact his sperm is in my vagina right now. Megan said oh wow my white pussy just got wet. I laughed out loud again.

Megan said I'll be right back with your food. Erin kissed me as Emma and Erin watched smiling too broadly. We talked until our food was ready. Megan brought out our delicious food. It smelt amazing and Megan said bon a pet tit. I said merci. She smiled and jiggled away with me admiring her sexy big booty.

We ate too much food. I was stuffed. I left the big tit waitress a huge tip and she hugged me tight. I was hard and she moaned whispering in my ears that my cock feels huge. We left the restaurant walking to the car when we heard music. Erin said let's go dance off this food.

Emily said hell yeah. We walked to the club next door. I paid for all four of us and walked in. It was packed. Erin got us a VIP booth. It was just the four of us. Emma and Emily were dancing with each other. Erin started grinding on my cock trying to make me hard. I became aroused in no time flat.

Erin said switch grabbing Emily and throwing her on me while she danced with Emma. I started grinding on Emily. She said your cock is hard. I said don't you like hard cocks anymore. Emily said you know I love your hard cock. I said good, are you wet yet. Emily said yeah, you know it's hard to control myself with you.

Erin switched again now I was grinding my hard cock on Emma's pussy. She said oh my god your dick is hard again. I said yeah, I know you like it Emma. She said oh yeah, I'm wet already.

We were dancing for a while when Erin pushed me on the couch and gave me a lap dance. I held her hips as she worked my cock up and down. Erin got up and sat Emily down on my lap. She gave me a lap dance for a while. Erin yanked her off and put Emma on my lap for a lap dance. I couldn't believe it. This was great and I was loving every minute of it.

Erin straddled me dry humping me and put her tits in my face. Erin got off and put Emily on my lap straddling my cock rubbing her big tits in my face. She liked it and so did I. Soon it was Emma's turn and she knew what to do straddling my cock and rubbing her big titties in my face.

Erin yanked her off and we all danced together until we were tired. We left before we fell asleep. Erin during the car ride said that was fun wasn't it. Emily said oh yeah lots of fun sorry about grinding on your boyfriend and putting my big tits in his face.

Erin said its ok, I don't mind, it was good fun. Emily said in that case I fucking loved it. Emma said I love it's too thanks for letting us play with your boyfriend, his big cock was hard the entire time. Emily said it sure was Erin.

Erin said did his big black cock make your white pussies wet. Emily said oh yeah very wet. Emma said it made my white pussy very wet too. Erin said he made all three of our white pussies wet tonight plus the big tit waitress. They all laughed out loud. I said she did moan when she felt my hard cock hugging me after my big tip.

Erin said I wonder if she likes black dick. Emma said I bet she wants one after tonight. Emily said I know I want one after tonight laughing. Erin said are you horny. Emily said oh yeah if my boyfriend was at my apartment, I'd fuck his brains out. Emma laughed and said same here.

I smiled and Erin had a naughty look in her eyes. We arrived back at our luxury apartment. Erin put on some dance music. She said let's keep this party going. Erin took off her dress, she had on red panties and bra. She said all of you guys are overdressed.

I took off my shirt and pants. Emily took off her dress leaving on her red panties and red bra. Emma said when in Rome. She took off her dress, she too had on red panties and bra. I said oh wow this is hot. I took off my boxers and all three of them saw my black bone at full attention. Emily said wow and Emma said damn. Erin smiled broadly at me.

Erin said now we are talking and took off her bra and panties. The two of us were naked. Emily took off her bra and panties. It forced Emma to take off her bra and panties too.

Erin started dancing on me, grinding on my cock with her wet pussy. I could feel its wetness on my cock shaft. Erin turned around and bent over working her ass up and down my cock. She stopped and said your turn Emily.

Emily happily danced up on me grinding on my cock as I massaged her ass. She turned around and worked my cock up and down with her juicy ass. I totally enjoyed my favorite roommate dancing with me oh natural.

Emma said my turn, Emily reluctantly gave up the dick. Emma grind her pussy on my cock then bent over and grind her juicy ass up and down my cock with pleasure.

Erin said who wants to share my boyfriend huge black cock in the forbidden dance. Emily said I do and to my surprise Emma said I do too.

Erin put me on the couch then straddled me sliding down my cock. I sucked her big tits as she rode my black pole with Emma and Emily watching biting their lips and very wet.

Erin said oh my god and her body vibrated as she spilled her pleasure milk on my cock. Erin got off and said your turn Emily. Emily happily straddled my cock and slid down it. I sucked on her big titties as she fucked my cock smiling ear to ear.

Emily screamed as she let her pleasure milk lubricate my cock. She kissed me passionately and my girlfriend Erin said now that's hot. Emily got off my cock. Emma slid down my pole then kissed me passionately. Erin said that hot. She started riding my cock and I sucked her big titties. I bit her nipples and it drove Emma over the edge.

Emma's body vibrated and she lubricated my black cock with her pleasure cream. She kissed me again and got off my cock. Erin got back on my cock kissing me passionately. She said time to make him cream.

Erin rode my cock hard until I ejaculated in her white pussy. After I lubricated Erin's pussy, she said that was a lot of fun then she said did you girls enjoy my boyfriend's big black cock.

Emily said I thoroughly enjoyed his big black cock deep in my white vagina until I lubricated it. Emma said I enjoyed the hell out of his big black cock deep in my white pussy. Erin said I always enjoy his big black cock in me especially when he ejaculates in me.

I said I enjoyed all three of your sweet white pussies. Erin said will you guys share my black stud with me again. Emma said hell yeah just don't tell my boyfriend. Emily said same here don't tell my boyfriend I'm giving it up to a black stud.

We moved the coffee table and laid down to sleep the rest of the night on the lush carpet. A week later, we went back to the same fancy restaurant and requested Megan to be our waitress. Our request for hot big tit Megan to be our waitress was granted.

We were sitting down and we decided to mess with her when she came over. I said hi Megan and she said hello sir. I got up and hugged her with my boner. Megan moaned again and I felt up her sexy juicy ass.

I sat down and Emily told Megan that he fucked all three of us. Megan said that's hot, he is a total stud. Megan was next to me so I reached between her sweet white thighs rubbing them. Megan moaned again trying to concentrate.

Erin took my hard-black cock out for Megan's viewing pleasure. Megan said oh my god that is a beautiful cock. Erin said do you want to taste it. Megan knelt down and started sucking my cock. I felt up her big titties as she blew me.

Emma said how about a quick hop on that big dick. Emily said do it girl, it's the best dick ever. Megan hiked up her skirt, moved her panties to the side and slid down my hard cock. She bounced up and down. I took her big tits out and sucked them as she fucked my black cock with her white pussy.

I said oh yeah baby, your white pussy feels so good on my black cock. Megan said oh yeah baby this is the best dick I've ever been on. She threw her head back and lubricated my cock with her pleasure cream. Megan kept fucking me and I felt that great feeling in my balls. I release my seed into Megan's tight ass white pussy.

I kissed her passionately and said thanks for the white pussy. Megan said your welcome and thanks for the big black dick. She got off my creamed boner, fixed her panties, pulled down her skirt and put away her big melons.

She told Erin thanks for sharing your boyfriends big black cock with me. Erin said my pleasure, it was hot watching you fuck his black cock. Emma and Emily said it was hot watching you give it up to a black man.

Megan said oh my god what have I done, please don't tell my husband I let you fuck my white pussy, he would kill my ass. I said your secret is safe with us baby. Erin, Emma and Emily said our lips sealed as stick sisters. Megan laughed out loud when they said it.

The end

www.ingramcontent.com/pod-product-compliance
Lightning Source LLC
LaVergne TN
LVHW020543160826
845677LV00015B/4173